Praise for
The Boxcar Children Beginning

"Indulging occasionally in foreshadowing and artfully incorporating details that will figure in later events, MacLachlan chronicles encounters and minor adventures on the farm in simple, straightforward language.... An approachable lead-in that serves to fill in the background both for confirmed fans and readers new to the series."—*Kirkus Reviews*

"Fans will enjoy this picture of life 'before,'..."—*Publishers Weekly*

"...series fans will like this glimpse into the Aldens' previous life."—*Booklist*

"The tone echoes the old-school charm of the original series, while short sentences, a straightforward plot, and plenty of dialogue make it an obvious choice for readers just transitioning into chapter books. Fans of the series will be pleased by this gentle addition, and others may very well be inspired to discover what lies in store for Henry, Violet, Jessie, and Benny."
—*The Bulletin of the Center for Children's Books*

"Sketchlike pencil illustrations throughout depict the many highs and lows of the siblings' tale and nicely complement MachLachlan's smooth, accessible narrative."—*The Horn Book Magazine*

"The innocence of the children is well captured through their straightforward dialogue, and each child has a distinct personality that will appeal to old fans and new readers of the series. Gently written, and harkening to a simpler time, this story will be an enjoyable family read and will serve as an easy-to-understand chapter book for emerging readers."—*School Library Journal*

THE BOXCAR CHILDREN BEGINNING

THE ALDENS OF FAIR MEADOW FARM

Library of Congress Cataloging-in-Publication Data

MacLachlan, Patricia.
The Boxcar children beginning : the Aldens of Fair Meadow Farm /
Patricia MacLachlan ; [interior illustrations by Robert Dunn].
    p. cm.
Prequel to the Boxcar children mysteries.
Summary: In the year before they become the orphans known as the
Boxcar children, Henry, Jessie, Violet, and Benny Alden live with their
parents at Fair Meadow Farm, where, although times are hard, they take
in a family who has been stranded in their car during a blizzard.
ISBN 978-0-8075-6616-9 (hardcover)
ISBN 978-0-8075-6617-6 (paperback)
[1. Families—Fiction. 2. Friendship—Fiction. 3. Brothers and sisters—Fiction.
4. Country life—Fiction.] I. Dunn, Robert, ill. II. Warner, Gertrude Chandler,
1890-1979. III. Title. IV. Title: Aldens of Fair Meadow Farm.
PZ7.M2225Bo 2012
[Fic]—dc23
2011051134

Cover illustration by Tim Jessell
Interior illustrations by Robert Dunn
Designed by Nick Tiemersma

10 9 8 7 6 5 4 3 2 1 LB 16 15 14 13

For information about Albert Whitman & Company,
visit our Web site at www.albertwhitman.com.

Table of Contents

This is for all the children—and in
memory of Gertrude Chandler Warner,
who wrote for them.—P.M.

THE BOXCAR CHILDREN BEGINNING

THE ALDENS OF FAIR MEADOW FARM

Patricia MacLachlan

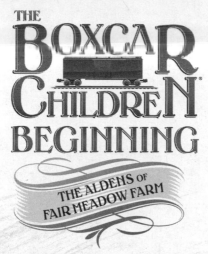

Based on the series created by
Gertrude Chandler Warner

Albert Whitman & Company
Chicago, Illinois

Chapter 1

Good Times

Henry stood in the doorway of the barn and looked out over the farm.

"I can smell spring," he said.

His younger sister Jessie leaned her pitchfork against the barn wall and stood next to him. There had been a spring snow in the night, but she could see grass. A thin layer of snow sat on the top of the Fair Meadow Farm sign that stood in their yard.

Jessie raised her head and sniffed.

Henry laughed.

"You look like Betty," he said.

Betty was one of their two cows. There was also Boots, who was mostly black and sweet and silent. But it was Betty who always stretched her neck out and put her nose in the air before she mooed. Papa called Betty "talkative."

Jessie smiled.

"It *is* spring," she said. "And I have my spring list."

Jessie took a piece of paper and a small hammer out of her pocket. She nailed the list to the wall.

Henry read over her shoulder.

"One: Make barn hideaway."

There was no number two.

"That's it?" asked Henry, grinning.

Usually Jessie's lists were longer.

"I've just started," said Jessie.

"What is a barn hideaway?" he asked.

"I'll show you," said Jessie. "Come."

Henry followed her to the ladder that went up to a loft. They climbed up. Bales of hay were stored there, in neat stacks.

Next to the hay was a small room with a door. The room was swept clean. There were two benches. There was a table with a vase with no flowers. A small, round window looked out over the next farm.

"A barn hideaway," said Jessie.

"It is," said Henry.

"Violet and Benny will like it," said Jessie. "Violet can do her sewing and painting up here. We can read books to Benny."

"And Benny can fall out the door and down the ladder," said Henry with a small smile. "We'll have to build a gate for Benny."

Jessie nodded.

"But he'll love it," she said.

Jessie frowned.

"I need more things for my list," she said.

They heard the sound of Papa's old gray car in the driveway.

Jessie and Henry climbed down the ladder and watched Papa walk up to the barn, carrying a cloth sack of nails and some boards for the stalls.

"Almost done?" he asked them.

"Just have to carry water for the cows," said Jessie.

Papa stood next to them.

"What are you looking at?"

"Spring," said Jessie and Henry together.

Their papa laughed.

"You're hopeful," he said. "There will be another good snowstorm before it is really spring. This is March!"

"Any news from town?" asked Jessie.

Papa sighed.

"Bad news. People losing their jobs and houses. Trying to find other places to make a living. Many people leaving. Hard times."

"You're lucky to have your job," said Henry.

"And Mama's baking for the market. It doesn't look like hard times here."

"I'm afraid you'll see hard times soon, Henry," said Papa.

"I don't want to see hard times," said Jessie.

"I don't want to, either," said Henry.

"No one does. We are lucky to have paying jobs, but it means more chores for you, though," said Papa, "being the oldest."

"And me," said Jessie.

"And you," Papa said.

"Everyone works at our house," said Jessie.

And that was true. Violet, who was ten, helped with the laundry and set and cleared the table at dinnertime. And Benny? Benny was just five and he made everyone smile.

"That's Benny's job," Mama had said, "to brighten our days."

The door to the house opened suddenly and Violet and little Benny ran out into the snow, followed by Mama.

Benny lay down in the snow, making a snow angel, and Violet started rolling spring snow for a snowman. Mama looked up at the barn and waved.

"Come play!" called Violet to Jessie and Henry.

Papa touched Henry.

"Go on," he said. "I'll finish here."

Henry and Jessie ran whooping down the hill, slipping and sliding in the snow.

"Watch out!" called Papa. "Mama has a snowball!"

Mama laughed.

"I do!"

In the paddock Betty stretched out her neck and mooed loudly.

"Moo," called Jessie.

"Moo," called Henry.

"Moo," said Benny, pointing at Betty.

Behind them, in the barn doorway, their papa smiled.

❧

It was nighttime. Henry was reading a book in bed, the lamplight falling across the pages.

"Henry?"

Jessie stood in the doorway.

Henry put the book down on the bedside table.

"What?"

"I'm worried about what Papa said. Hard times."

"Sometimes things happen we can't do anything about," said Henry.

"Maybe we have to find a way to do something," said Jessie. "I need a longer list. I need something exciting to add to it."

"Maybe something will happen," Henry said.

"It's too peaceful here," said Jessie. "Every day is like every other day."

As it turned out, something *would* happen.

Something not at all peaceful. Something Jessie and Henry could never have imagined.

It would happen the very next day.

Chapter 2

Hard Times

Papa had been right about snow. It was still winter. It had snowed all night and was still snowing. There was no sun.

"You were right," Jessie told Papa. "Right about winter."

"I'm right about lots of things," said Papa, making Mama laugh.

"No school for sure," said Mama.

"No one on the roads, either," said Papa. "Can't take bakery goods to market."

"That means a day off," Mama said happily.

Violet stirred oatmeal on the big stove.

"When I grow up I'm going to be a baker, like Mama," she said.

"You can be anything," said Mama. "Anything at all."

"Cow!" said Benny, making everyone laugh.

"I don't think Violet will be a cow," said Mama.

Henry put on his boots and coat and hat and went to the barn for chores. He put down new bedding in Betty's stall. Boots was still outside, but Betty liked the barn in winter. Henry could see his own breath in the air. He could see Betty's breath, too.

"Henry!" Jessie called from outside. She carried a pail of water for the cows. The wind took her hat, and her long hair blew around her face.

Henry ran down the hill and caught her hat, then followed her to the barn.

"I'm tired of winter," said Jessie.

Henry put her wool hat on her head.

"Remember how we loved the first snow?" he asked.

"I'll love this snow if it is the last one," said Jessie.

She carried the water into Betty's stall. She leaned against Betty.

"How can Betty be so *warm*?" she asked.

Henry leaned against Betty's other side. Betty rubbed her head against him.

"Get ready," said Henry.

They laughed. They knew Betty would moo in a minute.

Papa came into the barn, carrying a second pail of water.

That was when Betty mooed, the sound filling the barn.

"Hello, Miss Betty," said Papa. He went to the grain barrel and poured a scoopful of grain into Betty's bin. Boots came into the barn, snow-covered, her hooves clattering on the old wood floors. Papa scooped her some grain, too, and brushed snow off her.

Papa looked at the paper nailed to the wall.

"This must be a Jessie list," he said. "Where is this barn hideaway?"

Before Jessie could answer, Papa lifted his head.

"What's that?"

"Sounded like a car," said Henry.

"A car? No car can drive in these snowdrifts," said Papa.

He went to the barn door and looked out.

"Help! Help me, please!" It was a man's voice calling.

A car was stuck in the driveway snowdrift. The man was carrying a child.

Papa started running to the car.

"Henry, come with me! Jessie, tell Mama we'll need blankets!"

Jessie ran to the house, sliding in the snow. She opened the door, pushing it shut against the wind.

"Mama! People coming! We need blankets!" Mama turned from the stove and didn't stop to ask questions. She hurried to the bedroom and came out with blankets and bedcovers.

The door opened and there was a boy and girl, the girl carried by her father. Their mother looked frightened. In her arms was a small dog.

Mama took the mother's arm and pulled her to the wood stove in the kitchen. The dog jumped down.

"Is he all right here?" the woman asked Mama.

"Of course," said Mama.

She pulled a chair close to the stove.

"Here. Bring the child here."

"She's so cold," said the woman.

"Our car started to break down," said the man. "No heater. I've been looking for a house."

Mama smiled at them.

"You found one. I'll make some tea. Jessie, can you make hot chocolate for the children? Violet, get the cups, please. And a bowl of water for the dog."

"The dog is Joe," said the woman. "He won't be trouble."

Violet pulled a chair over to the counter and climbed up to get cups.

"Thank you," said the man. "I'm Jake Clark. This is my wife, Sarah. We lost our home and we were on our way to my sister's in New Hampshire. But the car . . ."

Jake Clark couldn't talk anymore. He was too upset.

"I'm Kate Alden," said Mama. "You met my husband, Ben, and son Henry. I think they're tending to your car. This is Jessie, Violet, and Benny."

Benny went over to sit next to Joe, who was drinking water. In a moment, Joe finished and looked at Benny.

"You're a beautiful dog," said Benny softly, patting Joe. "The most beautiful dog in the whole world."

Joe climbed up on Benny's lap, making Benny grin.

Sarah smiled at Benny. Then she spoke softly to Mama.

"I don't know what is going to happen to us," she whispered.

Mama poured tea and hot chocolate.

"You will stay with us," she said with a smile. "We'll make room for you until your car can be fixed. The children—what are your names?"

"I'm Meg," said the girl.

"William," said the boy.

"Well, Meg and William, you can share a room with Benny, Violet, Jessie, and Henry."

"We can hang blankets up on clotheslines," said Jessie excitedly. "Boys on one side, girls on the other."

"And Joe," said Benny.

"And Joe," said Jessie.

"That's a good idea, Jessie," said Mama. "Jessie is our organizer."

Meg, as cold as she was, smiled.

"You can go to school with us and you can help us with chores. We have cows to feed and stalls to clean. It will be fine," said Jessie. "We'll have fun, Mr. and Mrs. Clark. You'll see."

Jake Clark smiled.

"I think you should call us Jake and Sarah," he said, "since we're going to be family for a while.

"Our family will be bigger than it was," said Mama, reaching over and taking Sarah's hand.

"Just a little bigger," Mama said softly.

◦≈◦

When Henry came in with Papa after chores, he looked at Jessie, and they both knew that Papa had been right about things other than snow:

They would see hard times.

"So this is how hard times look," whispered Jessie to Henry.

"And something has happened to add to your list," said Henry.

Jessie put her hand in her pocket and felt the paper list.

"Yes, it has happened," she said. "It has. The Clarks have come from far away in the middle of a storm."

"In the middle of hard times," said Henry. "Nowhere for them to go. No home."

"Except Fair Meadow Farm," said Jessie.

She smiled at Henry.

"Our home."

Chapter 3

The Best Family of All

Ice and sleet came after the snow, making it hard to walk. Papa and Henry and Jake chopped out a path to the barn to feed and water the cows. Henry found a tarpaulin to put over Jake's car so it wouldn't ice up.

There was no school for two days, so most everyone stayed inside, listening to the wind and ice pellets on the windows and roof.

The children shared one large bedroom, hanging blankets on a clothesline across the room—the boys on one side, the girls on the other. Joe divided his time between the two, always ending up curled close to Benny.

"This is fun," said Meg.

"Were there other people on the road?" asked Henry.

William shook his head.

"In the city where we live, there were long lines of people standing in lines for soup and bread. There were old people and young people. Some babies were wrapped in blankets."

"I've never been to a city," said Jessie. "Are there tall buildings?"

"Very tall," said Meg. "And many, many people. There aren't any fields like here. There are no cows."

"When we left the city and drove into the country, most of the people who left their homes must have found shelter. Or maybe they drove on through the snow ahead of us," said William.

"It was scary," said Meg. "And sad. It was

like we were all alone in the world."

"Well, you're not," said Jessie. "And we'll do things so you won't be sad."

She took her list out of her pocket.

"What's that?" asked Meg.

"My list of things to do," said Jessie.

Jessie wrote:

2. Fix up bedrooms. Put up pictures.
3. Show Meg and William the hideaway.
4. Sew curtains for the hideaway.

"What's a hideaway?" asked Meg.

"You'll see tomorrow," said Jessie. "And we'll add lots of things to do to the list."

"I can sew curtains," said Meg.

"Me, too!" said Violet happily.

"Will you read to us, William?" asked Benny.

William was a great reader and was happy to see all their books.

"I left most of my books at home," he said.

He read them fairy tales and dog stories and

stories of heroes and horses with wings until Mama and Sarah came in to make sure the lights were off, and it was time for sleeping.

"I like the heroes," said Jessie.

"I like the horses with wings," said Violet.

"I like the dogs!" said Benny, Joe on his lap.

"I like the adventures," Henry said wistfully. "I'd like an adventure."

"Being here is an adventure for me," said Meg.

Henry smiled at her.

"I guess you're right."

"My mother said that life is a journey," said Meg. "And we're travelers."

∽∾

On Saturday the weather cleared and Mama went back to baking. In the kitchen she and Sarah were surrounded by bowls of batter, wooden spoons, and trays where buns were laid out. Row after row of buns for market. The children surrounded them, too. They spread the frosting on the buns—

even Benny, standing on a chair with his very small paintbrush.

"Not too much!" Mama said, wisps of hair loose from her hair clip. "These are buns with frosting, not frosting with buns!"

Sarah laughed as she took buns out of the oven.

"I think you'll need more sugar soon," she said.

"More sugar for sure," said Mama.

Henry chanted: "Sugar for sure. Sugar for sure."

The rest joined in: "Sugar for sure. Sugar for sure."

"Shigar, shigar, shigar," sang Benny.

Joe, under the table, was a smart dog. He knew something would be dropped, frosting or bun. He waited patiently, moving closer to Benny, who was more likely to drop anything. And sure enough, Benny couldn't wait any longer and took a bite out of a bun.

"Benny!" Jessie said loudly. "Not for eating! For the market!"

Surprised, Benny dropped the whole bun minus one bite. Joe leaped forward, scooped it up, and ran out into the parlor. Benny climbed down from the chair and ran after Joe.

"Benny, that's Joe's bun now. Come and frost another," called Mama.

Benny frowned.

"That was Benny's bun," he said, making them laugh.

"Let's stop for a bit and have some buns and tea," said Mama. "We've been working a long time."

"I'll cut them into small pieces, Kate," said Sarah. "You need six dozen for market, remember?"

Mama sat down and bushed her hair back out of her eyes.

"I do remember," Mama said wearily.

Sarah poured tea and Violet brought Mama the cup. A little hot water spilled on Violet's hand and she yelped, dropping the teacup on the floor. It broke in several pieces.

"Oh!" said Mama, her hands to her mouth.

Violet began to cry.

"Come, Violet," said Mama, opening up her arms. "It's only a teacup."

"But it was your favorite!" said Jessie.

Mama took Violet on her lap.

"It's only a teacup," she said to Violet. "It's just a thing. Don't forget that, Violet."

"But things are important," said Violet.

"Not as important as family and friends," said Mama. "I can always get another teacup. I can't get another you."

Sarah picked up the pieces of the flowered cup.

"What your mama says is true," said Sarah. "We had to leave many things we loved behind when we left."

"You brought Joe," said Violet, wiping tears away.

"We did," said Sarah. "Joe was more important than teacups."

"Maybe I can fix the cup," said Violet, getting off Mama's lap.

She wrapped the cup pieces in a handkerchief.

"If I had to leave home, I'd take my sewing bag," said Violet. "I have my own scissors and thread and glue. And sewing needles."

Mama smiled.

"Violet is our mender and fixer."

"I'd take Joe," said Benny.

"But Joe doesn't belong to you, Benny," said Henry.

Benny thought.

"Then I'd take Bear," he said. He held his worn stuffed bear under his arm.

"I took my doll," said Meg. The doll looked like Meg, the two of them with black curly hair. "And a box of crayons."

"I took three books," said William. "Only three," he added in a soft, sad voice. "I read them over and over."

"What would you take if you had to leave?" Jessie asked her mama.

"I'd take you!" said Mama. "All of you. You are the most important. The best family of all!"

Jessie and Henry smiled at each other. They didn't know if they were the best family of all, but they liked Mama saying so.

"Bear says he wants a bun," said Benny.

They laughed for now. They had no way

of knowing it, but they were all to remember this talk later. They would remember Mama's words—the best family of all.

Much later.

∽✎✎

And that night, while everyone was sleeping, Violet carefully glued the pieces of her Mama's rose teacup together. She set it on the windowsill in the kitchen.

If she didn't look too closely, it almost looked the way it always had. Almost.

Chapter 4

School and Songs

The snow melted quickly, only small fields of ice left behind. Henry, Jessie, Violet, William, and Meg walked along the road to school. Benny had stayed home.

"I'll take care of Joe," Benny called.

He waved good-bye to them. It was already sunny.

"How far?" asked William.

"A mile," said Henry.

"More or less," added Jessie, grinning.

Henry laughed.

"That's what our papa says. More or less."

"It's more when it's cold and there's wind," said Jessie. "Less on a spring day."

Spring birds had returned early and they swooped back and forth over the road. They could see a flock of robins in the grass.

The next farm had a fenced meadow with horses and cows. A small house was tucked next to a stand of trees. Smoke came from the stone chimney.

Meg stopped suddenly.

The others walked a few feet before they realized it.

"What's wrong?" asked Jessie.

"I'm scared," said Meg. "A new school. A new teacher and a new class."

Jessie walked back and took Meg's hand.

"Mr. Miller is used to new students. He's nice. You'll like him. And we're half the class right here."

Their neighbor, Rubin, rode his horse, Mike, along the fence.

"On your way to school?" he asked. "I used to walk this very same road to the very same school when I was a boy. Down the hill, around the pond, and on to school."

Henry smiled and reached up to stroke Mike's nose.

"This is Meg and William Clark," said Jessie. "Their car broke down in the storm. They're part of our family now until they can get their car fixed. This is Rubin Barnes."

"Hello, Mr. Barnes," said William.

"Call me Rubin."

"Hello, Rubin," said Meg. "Did you live here when you were a boy?"

"I was born here," said Rubin. "In that house, in the bedroom where my wife and I sleep."

"Think of that," Meg said slowly. "Living all your life where you were born. We're moving because we lost our home."

"They're travelers," said Violet.

"Sorry," said Rubin. "But you'll find a new place. There are always good places."

"We have a good place right now," said William.

"You certainly do," said Rubin. "Well, you can come over and ride my horses anytime you want."

"I'd like that," said Meg.

"Better get to school," said Rubin. Then he trotted off across the field.

They began walking down the road again, around a small pond. There were small patches of ice along the edges of the pond, some ducks swimming in the middle.

"I'm glad we stopped at your house," said Meg.

"Me, too," said William.

"Me, too," said Violet and Jessie and Henry all at once.

Henry laughed.

"If Betty were here, she'd moo."

And as it turned out, Meg and William liked Mr. Miller. Meg was good at numbers and he asked her to help the younger children. He lent William three books to take home.

"The walk home from school seems shorter," said William, carrying his books.

"More or less," said Violet, making them all laugh.

&

Jake was a fixer.

"He was a handyman before there was no more work," said Sarah.

He fixed the windows that stuck. He fixed two chairs and a table leg on the kitchen table. He fixed the barn door latch so that the door didn't blow open and shut in the wind anymore. Violet watched him carefully because she was a fixer, too.

"Here," Jake said to Violet. "This is a little screwdriver for you. I have an extra one."

"Thank you," said Violet. "I'm glad you're here."

"I'm glad you're here, too, " Papa told him. Papa was a carpenter, but he didn't always have time to fix things at his own house.

"I'm glad, too," said Jake.

And then Jake fixed Mama's old piano in the parlor.

"It works now," he told Mama. "Go on. Play."

When Mama sat down and started playing, there were tears at the corners of her eyes.

"This was my mother's piano," she said. "She played every single evening of her life."

Mama played "Over the Rainbow" and "Good Night Irene" and "Pennies from Heaven." Sarah and Jake danced and Joe barked. She played "Tea for Two" and "On the Good Ship Lollipop" until the soup boiled over in the kitchen and everyone ran in to clean up and eat dinner.

In the middle of dinner, William looked up at everyone around the table.

"Could this be our new home?" he asked in a soft voice.

It was very quiet then. No one speaking, no clattering of spoons or forks against plate, only a soft quiet woof from under the table. Joe was reminding everyone to drop food.

Finally Mama spoke.

"This will be your home until your father

can get the parts to fix the car. It may not always be your home, William, but . . ."

Papa finished her sentence.

"But we will always be your family."

William smiled.

"Family," he said.

Joe woofed under the table.

"Joe said 'family'!" said Benny. "I know he did. I know woof talk!"

"I think you're right, Benny," said William very seriously. "I'm *sure* you're right."

"I am," Benny said happily.

Chapter 5

Differences

The days marched one after the other into a warm and wet spring.

Every day the children walked to school and home again.

Every day Benny stayed home with Joe.

Every day there were chores. Henry and William carried water and cleaned out the cow stalls. Meg and Jessie laid down new hay and filled the grain bins. They had a contest to see how long it would be before Betty mooed.

"Chores are fun," said Meg.

"They're more fun with you two here," said Henry.

All of them liked the barn hideaway. They brought out old blankets to make hay beds. They painted pictures for the walls.

"We can't bring Benny here without a gate at the top," said Meg. "He could fall down the ladder."

So, while they set the table with dishes and put flowers in the empty vase, Violet sewed a bright flowered curtain for the window. And Jake built them a gate with a latch so Benny could play there with them.

One night they slept there, William and Meg, Henry and Jessie, and Benny without Joe, because Joe did not like being high up in the barn. Benny slept with Bear instead.

They read books until there was no light.

Then they whispered in the dark.

"What's that sound?" asked Meg.

"Probably a mouse," said Henry.

"Or a giant rat!" said William.

Suddenly, in the darkness, Betty mooed,

the sound bouncing off the wooden walls of the barn, the noise so loud they all screamed and then laughed until all was quiet again.

Every day Sarah and Mama baked goods for the market in town.

And every day Jake Clark went to town with Papa, waiting for the parts to his car to arrive so he could fix it. Every day he came back empty-handed.

"I wish *I* could fix it," said Violet.

Jake smiled at her.

"If anyone could, you could," he said. "You're a very good fixer. But this needs a special part that we can't make."

He looked at Papa.

"I'm sorry. We've been here for quite a time."

"No matter, Jake," said Papa. "You've done your own share of fixing, and I thank you. It will come when it comes."

"Look!" said Violet.

Out in the meadow Meg was riding Betty, holding on to a rope around Betty's neck. She leaned over and said something to Betty, and Betty began walking faster.

"Is that safe?" asked Jake, looking worried.

"Betty's quiet and kind," said Papa. "But I have to admit I've never seen anyone ride her."

"Betty and Meg are good friends," said Violet.

"I'll say," said Jake

"And I can't say I've ever seen *anyone* ride *any* cow before, either!" said Papa.

Jake and Papa began laughing as Betty walked around the meadow, looking like a fairly fat horse, Meg leaning over to whisper in Betty's ear.

Jessie and Henry came out of the barn to lean on the meadow fence and watch. Mama, Sarah, William, and Benny came out the front door of the house.

Meg waved.

"Jake," called Sarah. "Is that safe?"

"Betty's a gentle cow, Sarah," he called back to her. "Not a bucking bronco. I'm about to do something much more dangerous. I'm going to climb up on the barn and patch the roof. *That's* dangerous."

"I'll give you a kiss when you come down," said Sarah, laughing.

Jake smiled.

"Look!" called Violet, pointing at Meg. Betty was going faster and faster!

"I do believe that old Miss Betty is galloping," said Papa, squinting his eyes in the sunlight.

"Cowgirl!" shouted Benny, making everyone laugh.

In the meadow, Betty stretched out her neck and mooed.

Even Benny laughed this time.

⌘

The days grew longer. After chores, everyone played outside until dinnertime—kick the can and hide-and-seek—shrieking happily in the fading light. Violet was the best at hiding, except for Jake, who came out to play, too. No one could find him until an hour later when Violet found him sleeping in the backseat of his car.

"Now it's really spring," said Henry. "Smell it?"

It was true. You could smell it. The grass was green, the trees budded, splashes of yellow forsythia.

"It's almost school vacation. Let's do something special," said Jessie.

"Special things cost money," said Henry.

"There's cookie jar money," said Benny.

"But that is for emergencies," said Mama. "For something you really, really need. You all know that."

"Something special . . . something that doesn't cost money," said Meg. "We'll think of something. We will."

"Something happy and fun," said Jessie. "What makes us happy?"

"Cows," said Benny.

"Laughing," said Violet.

"Well, we all laugh when we're happy," said

Henry. "That makes you laugh."

"Clowns," said Violet.

"When have you ever seen a clown?" asked Jessie.

"Cows," repeated Benny, making them all laugh.

"I have *heard* of clowns," said Violet.

"Well," said William, looking pleased with himself, "I remember something that made you happy, Meg."

He leaned over and whispered in her ear.

"Oh!" Meg's eyes widened. "Yes!"

"What?" asked Henry and Jessie at the same time.

"I'll tell you later! A secret!" said Meg. "But it will make you happy. It will make you laugh."

∽◆∾

It was evening and William had just finished reading *Little Red Riding Hood* to Benny. A picture fell out of the book.

"Who's that?" asked Jessie.

"Our grandfather," said William. "When we go to our new home, we'll live with him."

Violet picked up the picture.

"He looks nice," she said.

"He is," said Meg. "Do you have a grandfather?"

Jessie and Henry quickly looked at each other.

"We do," said Henry.

"But we don't see him," said Jessie.

"He doesn't like us," said Benny.

Behind them, Mama made a sound. She stood in the doorway.

"But that's not true, Benny," she said.

"He doesn't," said Benny stubbornly.

"Why doesn't he see us?" asked Violet.

Mama sat down next to Benny.

"Well, he and your papa had some differences," she said.

"What kind of differences?" asked Henry.

"What are 'differences'?" asked Benny.

Mama didn't speak for a moment.

"Well, your grandfather wanted us to live

with him in his big house. We wanted to live here. On my family's farm."

She sighed.

"He was disappointed."

"So he doesn't want to see us?" asked Violet.

"He's stubborn," said Mama.

"He hates us," said Benny.

"That's not true, Benny. If . . . *when* he sees you, he'll love you. Believe me when I say that."

She stood up.

"Do you believe me?" she asked.

Jessie, Henry, and Violet nodded.

"Yes," said Benny.

"Lights out, now," Mama said.

The lights went out. It was quiet for a time. Joe came to curl up next to Benny. Benny put his arm around Joe.

"We won't see him," said Benny in the darkness.

Chapter 6

A Small Dot in a Big World

On the last day of school, Papa brought home a treasure. At least it was a treasure to Henry.

It was a globe of the world that turned on a wooden stand.

"I found it by the road, next to a house that people had left."

The globe showed the different countries and the oceans and rivers. Henry showed Violet where they lived.

"Right there!" he said, pointing.

"The world sure is big," said Violet. "We

live in a small dot in a big world."

"Where did you live, William?" asked Henry.

William slowly turned the globe.

"There." He pointed.

"Your city is a big dot in the world," said Violet.

Every so often, Violet reached over to touch the dot that was the town where they lived.

Meg and Jessie whispered excitedly.

"What are you whispering about?" asked Henry.

"A secret for now," said Jessie. "We'll tell you later."

And that night, in their bedroom, with the blanket hung between them and the lights out, the globe sitting on Henry's desk, the secret was out. They whispered and laughed until Mama and Papa came in, Sarah and Jake behind them.

"What's going on in here?" Mama asked. "You have chores in the morning."

"We're planning something exciting," said Meg.

"Something to make us all happy," said Violet.

"What?" asked Papa.

"A circus!" said Violet, grinning. "We'll have animals and clowns and costumes and juggling . . ."

"I can juggle," said Henry.

"I can sew costumes," said Violet.

"And what about animals?" asked Jake.

"There's Joe!" said Benny.

"And Betty," said Meg. "I will get Betty ready for the circus."

"Ready?" said Sarah. "What do you mean, 'ready'?"

"You'll see," said Jessie.

"You'll see," said Henry.

"What will I do?" asked William.

"You'll see!" the children said together, laughing.

"And who will be a clown?" asked Jake.

"You'll see!" they all said, shrieking with happiness.

Benny fell backward on the bed in an

excited heap. Joe licked his face.

"We'll invite Rubin and Belle. That's his wife. And his grandchildren are visiting. And Thomas and Elliot from down the road. Remember? They're in our class at school. Everyone can come!" said Jessie. "Maybe we could sell tickets."

"No tickets," said Papa, shaking his head. "No one has money for such things."

"*We* can't even afford tickets," said Jake with a smile.

"Then it will be a free circus!" said Violet. "I can't wait. The very first free circus in town!"

Mama laughed.

"You'll have to wait until tomorrow for planning. Go to sleep! Hush, everyone."

There was quiet in the bedroom after Mama, Papa, Sarah, and Jake left.

Joe yawned a dog yawn with a squeak at the end. It was still quiet.

"I like living in this small dot of a town," said William after a while.

"So do I," said Meg.

"Do you, Henry? Jessie?" asked Meg.

There was silence.

Henry and Jessie were asleep.

More silence.

And then Benny whispered.

"I do."

Chapter 7

Betty Joins the Circus

It was vacation, but everyone was up. Everyone was busy.

Jessie unrolled her very long list. It almost touched the floor.

"My list has grown!"

"I'll say," said Henry, laughing.

Jessie read the list out loud.

"Circus List. One: Costumes for clowns? Who will the clowns be? Two: How do we make clown wigs? Yarn? Does Mama have yarn? Three: How do we make an elephant trunk? Paper?"

"Papa's big, gray winter socks!" shouted Benny.

"Benny's right. We can stuff them," said Violet. "Then sew up the ends," said Meg.

"What if he's wearing them?" asked William.

"We'll tickle him and take them away!" said Benny.

Everyone laughed.

"Can I be the animal trainer?" asked Benny.

Jessie smiled.

"What do you know about animal training?" she asked.

Benny stood up.

"Come, Joe," he said.

Joe came and sat in front of Benny.

Benny held out his arm.

"Go," said Benny.

Joe jumped over Benny's arm, turned around, and jumped over again.

Jessie was so surprised she couldn't speak. So was Meg.

"I never ever saw Joe do a trick in his whole

life," said Meg.

"Well, he does tricks now," said William. "I think we should vote Benny as the animal trainer!"

"Yay!" said Benny.

"Yay!" they all said.

❧

Mama and Sarah baked for the circus party. Papa and Jake worked on the barn roof, and the children worked, too.

Violet sewed in the bedroom.

Meg worked with Betty behind the barn where no one could see.

"What is she doing?" asked Sarah.

"Don't know," said Jake. "It's a secret."

"Even from us?" asked Sarah.

"*Mostly* from us," said Jake.

Benny and Joe worked in the backyard, Joe happy with bites of leftover dinner.

Henry juggled with three and four cloth balls sewn and stuffed by Violet.

Jessie and William sat with their heads close

to each other, writing and laughing secret things.

The list grew longer.

Two days of this.

Their neighbor Rubin came by.

"I hear there is an event," he called up to Papa and Jake, who were hammering shingles on the barn roof.

"There is," called Papa. "How did you know?"

"There's a sign on my fence post," said Rubin.

Papa and Jake laughed.

"You coming?" asked Papa.

"I wouldn't miss it," said Rubin. "Belle is coming. The grandchildren, too. We'll bring cookies and a jug of lemonade."

"Bring a chair for Belle, too," said Papa.

Rubin laughed.

"And one for me."

❧

Mama and Sarah brought trays of sandwiches out under the red maple tree for lunch. They spread blankets on the ground.

"Do you have lunch for us, too?" asked Papa, coming down the barn ladder.

"For all of us," said Mama.

Jake came down the ladder, too, Joe running over to leap up to bite his shoes.

"Joe! I'll fall!" said Jake, laughing.

Jake jumped down from the ladder and Sarah kissed him.

"I promised you I'd do that," she said.

"You did," said Jake, blushing.

Under the tree was cool and quiet.

Joe stretched out and eyed Benny's sandwich.

"Papa?" said Violet. "I need a wooden box."

"What for?"

"Secret."

"How big?" asked Jake.

Violet held her hands out and made the shape of a big square.

"Aha!" said Jake.

"What does *aha* mean?" asked Violet.

"It means I have one in my car. I keep tools in it."

Violet smiled.

"Could I borrow it?"

"You bet."

"One more day," said Henry.

"One more day!" they echoed.

Papa reached out to give Joe a bite of his sandwich.

"One more day," he whispered to Joe. "Give

me a smile, Joe."

Joe sat up and cocked his head to one side. His tongue hung out.

"Joe *always* smiles," Benny said.

Wind rustled the leaves of the tree. Sun filtered down over them all. And from the side meadow, Betty looked at them all. She walked to the fence.

"Betty's going to moo," said Jake in a low voice.

And she did.

Chapter 8

Circus!

Circus day at last! It was sunny and dry.

No child was in sight, except for Violet. Her sewing was done.

Sarah and Mama carried out kitchen chairs and lined them up for the audience. Papa had brought balloons from town, and Violet tied them to the chairs.

They floated like colorful clouds.

"I wonder where Jake is," said Sarah.

"Where's Jake?" Mama asked Violet.

"He'll be along in a bit," said Violet with a smile.

"Secrets," said Mama. "And where are the others?"

"In a bit," repeated Violet.

"And Joe?" asked Sarah.

Violet took a breath.

"In a bit," they all said together, laughing.

Rubin and Belle came with their own chairs and two grandchildren. Thomas and Elliot came riding their horse.

Two families from town came, waving the signs that had been tacked on fence posts. And there were others, including a big, friendly brown dog, who sat quietly.

Sarah and Mama served lemonade and cookies. Then everyone sat.

A curtain had been strung from the maple tree to the barn. Suddenly it opened! Jessie and Meg scurried out of the way, making everyone laugh.

And there was Henry, wearing a jacket with gold buttons and the black hat his father had worn on his wedding day. He had a small whip made from twisted leather. He snapped it.

"Welcome, ladies and gentlemen!" he said loudly. "Welcome, children!"

"And dog!" said Thomas in the audience.

"And dog," said Henry, grinning.

The audience applauded. Elliot put his fingers to his lips and whistled. Jessie and Meg peeked out from the curtain.

"Welcome to our free circus," Jessie whispered loudly.

"The writer-director speaks," said Mama to Papa.

"The boss," said Papa with a smile.

"Welcome to our free circus!" called Henry. "Put your money away! You will see wondrous and amazing things here: jugglers, dancers, acrobats! Clowns, trained dogs, and the most stupendous surprise of all: an elephant! And a small surprise!"

The audience applauded and looked at one another in amazement.

"An elephant?" Mama said to Papa.

Papa shook his head.

"Wait and see," Papa said.

"But first of all, we present Jake-O and Jess, our clowns!"

Henry snapped his whip. The curtain opened again. And there was Jake with a yarn wig and a huge dress. Jessie was dressed in a suit.

"Where did that suit come from?" asked Mama.

"Your closet," said Violet.

"That's my marriage suit!" said Papa.

Sarah laughed at the sight of Jake doing a cartwheel, the dress hanging like curtains around him.

"Those are my old curtains," said Mama.

"Oof," said Jake as he clumsily landed his cartwheel. His yarn wig tilted and covered his face.

The audience laughed and applauded.

Jessie and Jake ran around after each other, then collided in the middle, falling down, their feet in the air.

The audience laughed again.

Jessie and Jake-O bowed and fell over again. More laughter.

Jessie and Jake blew kisses to everyone and left.

"I don't believe this," said Sarah with a smile.

"Ladies and gentlemen," said Henry, snapping his whip, "the amazing, the spectacular Princess Meg riding bareback on her worthy steed!"

"What steed?" asked Sarah.

Out came Betty, colorful paper flowers around her neck. Meg, dressed in filmy fabric, a gold paper crown on her head, waved at the audience, and the audience waved back at her. "Yay, Betty!" called Rubin, who had always loved Betty.

Betty plodded slowly around the lawn, her wet, black eyes bright in the sunlight. All of a sudden, Meg got to her knees on Betty's back. And then Meg stood up, her dress's filmy fabric flying out behind her as Betty began to run, then gallop.

Meg held on to the rope with one hand and waved with the other.

The audience howled and clapped.

Meg jumped down from Betty and bowed. The paper flowers fell from Betty's neck and she began to eat them.

The audience laughed as Betty looked at them, flowers hanging out of her mouth.

"And now for . . ." said Jessie from behind the curtain.

"I know. I know. And now for a great treat!" said Henry. "The young trainer with Joseph!"

"Who's Joseph?" asked Mama.

But before anyone could answer, out came Benny, pulling his wagon with Jake's toolbox on top.

"Hi, Mama!" he called, waving.

The audience clapped.

Benny stopped.

"Bow!" called Jessie.

Benny grinned and bowed.

And then he opened the box, and out jumped Joe!

"Joseph," said Papa laughing.

Joe ran around the box and yard. And then Benny picked up a stick and held it out straight.

"Jump!" said Benny.

Joe jumped over the stick.

Cheering and applause.

"I never knew Joe could do that," said Sarah.

Benny picked up a circle hoop.

"Hush everyone," said Henry. "This is very difficult and needs complete silence!"

"Or a snack," said Papa.

Everyone grew quiet.

Benny held up the circle.

"Now, Joe!" said Benny.

Joe sat.

"Now, Joe!" repeated Benny.

Joe looked.

Henry put his hand in his pocket and took out some dog snacks. He handed them to Benny.

Benny held them up, and Joe happily jumped through the hoop, then when Benny turned, jumped again, and then again.

He sat.

Benny gave him a snack.

Then Joe jumped through the last hoop and up onto the box.

Benny bowed.

Everyone clapped and whistled.

And Benny rolled Joe out of the yard and behind the curtain.

"And now," said Henry, snapping his whip, "for our final act." He looked quickly behind the curtain.

"Wait just a minute," he added, "while we get the elephant and the small surprise ready!"

The audience was suddenly quiet.

"Ready?" asked Henry.

"Ready," came a voice from behind the curtain.

"The master elephant trainer with a surprise!" Henry announced proudly.

The curtain opened and in came the elephant, led by William. The elephant was Boots, with a gray blanket and a stuffed elephant trunk.

"My socks!" said Papa. "I wondered where they were!"

"Elephant!" cried one of Rubin's grand-children.

"That's Boots," cried another child.

"Elephant!" called the audience.

And then the elephant was followed by a tiny gray-blanketed creature. It was the small surprise.

"A baby elephant!" cried a child.

It was Joe with a stuffed-sock trunk. He walked behind Boots, his trunk bouncing in front of him, while everyone clapped.

And then it was over. They all came out to take their bows: Jake-O and Jess, the clowns, Princess Meg with Betty, Benny with Joe in his

wagon, and William, the elephant trainer. The group called for Violet, who came running to join them.

They bowed in a row. Boots, as always, was sweet and silent.

The audience applauded.

"This is the best day of my life," said William.

Betty mooed.

The friendly brown dog got up and went home.

The circus was over.

Chapter 9

The Day After

Henry, Jessie, Violet, Meg, and William sat on a blanket under the maple tree. Benny was there, too, but he had fallen asleep after the long circus day. Joe stretched out beside him.

Papa had driven his car to town early to deliver buns to the bakery and check the mail.

"You were wonderful, all of you," said Mama.

"Your costumes were fine, Violet," said Sarah.

"Meg helped," said Violet.

"And my box has a new cover now," said Jake. "Did you do that?"

Violet smiled.

"I used the small screwdriver you gave me. And Papa helped me cut a board the right size."

"Thank you, Violet."

"You're welcome. You were a funny clown, Jake."

"Thank you again, Violet. Jessie was a good clown partner," said Jake. "It took lots of practice for us to learn how to fall down together."

Everyone laughed.

"Betty was good," said Meg.

"You were good," said Sarah. "Henry, you were a great announcer. You had to make it all work."

"Maybe when I grow up I'll be a circus announcer," said Henry.

"I'd say, by the look of your globe inside, that you'll be an explorer," said Jake.

Henry thought.

"I like that," he said, smiling. "An explorer."

"The chief explorer," said Jake.

"I like 'chief,' too," said Henry.

"I loved being an elephant trainer," said William. "I really did. You know, there was a time yesterday when I really, really believed Boots was an elephant. And Joe!"

And then William repeated what he had said the day before.

"It was the best day of my life."

They all looked up as Papa drove his gray car up the dirt road to the driveway. For a moment, Papa didn't get out of the car. He just sat there in the car. Then, slowly, he opened the door and got out. He walked over to them. He carried a package.

He held the package out for Jake.

"Your part came," he said.

⟜⟝

Everything changed that morning.

In the heads of all the children, nothing was the same.

There would be no more walking to school together and playing tag all the way home.

No more stories of heroes and winged horses, even when the lights were out.

No more sleeping in the barn hideaway.

No more frosting buns in the kitchen.

No more watching Meg's hair flying out behind her as she rode Betty.

No more circuses.

When Benny woke up and they told him, he burst into tears. He clutched Joe in his arms, rocking back and forth.

When Sarah saw that, she burst into tears, too.

"We won't be far away," said Sarah. "You will come and visit us."

She wiped her eyes and wrote down an address on a piece of paper.

"Here is where we'll be. Where should I put this so you can find it when you need it?"

"The cookie jar with our money," said Jessie. "That's the safest place."

"That is what I will do," said Sarah. "Don't

forget. We are in the cookie jar!"

This made the children smile even though they were sad.

"Jake won't be able to leave today," said Papa. "Maybe you can fill up today with fun."

No one spoke.

"Chores first, of course," Papa said cheerfully. "Go on, go on!"

Henry, Jessie, Meg, and William all went to the barn. Benny and Joe followed behind.

Violet went to watch Jake work on the car engine. The hood was folded back, and when she bent over to look, Jake turned his head to look at her for a moment. Then he went back to work.

The barn was dark and cool and quiet.

Joe jumped into a pile of bedding hay. Benny sat with him.

"I'd like to put the smell of this barn into a little jar and take it with me," said Meg.

No one said anything.

Henry and William began to shovel old hay out of the stalls and throw it out the back door in a pile.

"Maybe the car part won't work," whispered Jessie to Meg. "Maybe the car won't start."

Meg smiled.

"That would be nice."

Betty walked into the barn and came over to where Meg stood. Betty nosed Meg's shoulder, rubbing her long face there.

Meg's eyes filled with tears.

"I'll miss this old cow," she said. "And you

can't put Betty in a jar for me to take along."

Jessie put her arms around her.

"We will always be friends," said Jessie.

"We will always be family," said Meg.

Suddenly there was the sound of a car starting outside. Henry and William looked up and stopped working. Meg and Jessie looked at the barn door.

Violet stood there.

"Jake fixed the car," she said sadly.

Chapter 10

Not Good-Bye

The children slept late the next morning, almost as if they were sleeping so no one would leave. William and Meg wouldn't get into the car. No one would wave good-bye. Everything would stay the same.

Jake and Sarah, Mama and Papa were at the kitchen table, drinking coffee. They were quiet.

There were several suitcases by the front door, and some boxes.

"Who wants cocoa?" asked Mama. "We have pancakes, too."

William sat down at the table. He shook his head.

"I'm not hungry," he said. "Thank you," he added.

Meg and Jessie and Violet sat down. They looked at one another and shook their heads, too.

"I'm not saying good-bye," said Benny, getting up on his chair.

There was a silence. Then Benny smiled.

"Not good-bye," he said. "It is a not good-bye day!"

Everyone looked at him.

"And I'm hungry for pancakes," he added.

"Benny," said Papa, "that is a brilliant idea!"

"It is?" said Benny.

"It is," said Papa. "You're the smartest person here."

"I am?"

Benny looked amazed.

"Papa's right," said Henry. "We won't say good-bye because we'll see each other again soon. I'm hungry, too!"

"Me, too," said Meg.

"Me, too," said the others.

"Well," said Mama, "let's have a very splendid breakfast."

"And we won't say good-bye!" said Violet.

"And remember," said Jessie, "Jake and Sarah, Meg and William are in the cookie jar!"

"Joe, too," said Benny.

"And Joe!" said everyone.

The breakfast was long and noisy, with lots of laughter.

And when Jake and Sarah packed up the car, and Meg and William packed their things, Henry showed William and Meg where they were going to live on the turn-around globe.

"There," he said. "You're only this far."

He held out his fingers to measure.

"Only this far. Three inches away."

"Not good-bye," said William and Meg outside.

"Not good-bye," said everyone.

It was Joe who now looked sad, walking to

the car with Meg and William, turning to look back at Benny as if waiting for him.

"It's all right, Joe. Not good-bye, Joe," said Benny, his eyes beginning to fill with tears.

"Remember the cookie jar," called Sarah, waving.

And they were gone.

Chapter 11

Summer

It was very quiet at Fair Meadow Farm. Everything seemed to move more slowly, silently.

Henry and Jessie missed their walks to school with Meg and William. Benny missed Joe.

"I'd like to have Joe," he told Mama.

"Well, Joe belongs to another family," she said. "Maybe when we have enough money to feed a dog, we'll get one."

"When I am grown up, I will have twenty-seven dogs," said Benny.

"That's a lot," said Mama.

"Twenty-seven," said Benny proudly.

Now, at night, Benny slept with Bear.

∽∾

School ended and it was a hot summer. Other people who'd lost their jobs and houses came by the Alden farm. A family lived out in the meadow in their tent for a while. A man and his wife stayed in their car for a week. The man had a guitar, and some summer evenings at dusk, they would hear his soft music.

"Hard times," Henry said to Jessie.

"I hope the hard times end," said Jessie.

But they didn't that summer.

And one day a man and his wife stopped, looking for the hospital. His wife was about to have a baby.

"The hospital is in the next town over," said Mama. She looked closely at the woman.

"What's your name?" she asked.

"Milly," said the woman. "My husband's Matt."

"Well, Milly, I think you're not going to make it to the hospital. You'd better come into the house."

And that night, in Mama and Papa's bedroom, a baby boy was born. His name was Thomas.

Benny was happy to have someone younger than he was. He sang to Thomas and told him stories.

"Could Thomas sleep with me?" he asked Milly.

Milly smiled.

"I wish he could, Benny," she said. "He's a little young for that."

"And Thomas isn't a dog," said Violet.

"I wish you all lived with me," said Milly. You are the very best family in the world."

"You are," said Matt.

"When Thomas is older I will tell him about that wonderful place where he began his life," said Milly.

"I could be Uncle Benny," said Benny.

"You *are* Uncle Benny," said Matt.

After a week, Milly, Matt, and Thomas left. And it was quiet again.

Rubin came over and cut the first crop of hay, and when it dried, Henry and Jessie and Papa gathered it for winter storage. He gave Rubin half for his work.

The next day, when Papa came back from town, he had a letter from Meg and William.

Dear Henry, Jessie, Violet, and Benny,
  We are here! The car worked. Papa is a great fixer. We live in a house big enough for all of you, with our aunt and our grandfather. You're invited to come anytime. Remember, we are only three inches away. And we are family.
  Papa has some work as a handyman, and William is working at a farm for the summer. There is a nice cow there that the farmer won't let Meg ride.
  We miss you! And tell Benny that Joe will be very happy when Benny comes to visit. He likes sleeping with Benny more than us. He told us so in woof talk.
  Love to all,
  William and Meg
  PS Kiss Betty on the nose for Meg.

"William and Meg like their new place," said Jessie.

"It must have been hard to leave their old place, though," said Henry.

"I wouldn't like to leave here," said Violet. "They're brave."

"I wish we had a grandfather to visit," said Benny.

No one said anything.

"You will one day," said Papa. "You will."

There was another silence. Mama looked at Papa.

"Will he get me a dog?" asked Benny.

Papa smiled.

"He might do that," he said.

"We'll go visit William and Meg sometime," said Mama.

"Sometime," said Papa. "But it is a long way."

"Three inches only," said Violet.

"Three inches is much longer in real life than it looks on the globe," said Mama.

"And I will *not* kiss Betty on the nose!" said Papa, making them all smile.

Chapter 12

A Spool of Thread

"Summer is almost over," said Henry in the barn. "School will start soon. I smell fall."

Jessie laughed.

"I remember you saying the same thing about last spring," she said. "And then it snowed."

"I did say that," said Henry. "And you stretched out your neck like Betty and said you smelled it, too."

Jessie stretched out her neck and smelled.

"I don't smell fall yet. I think there's more summer to go."

Papa tooted his funny-sounding car horn for Mama.

Mama carried trays of cookies and biscuits out to the car to deliver. Papa opened the door for her, and she set them on the backseat.

"We'll be back this afternoon," she called. "Do you want anything in town, Lambs?"

Henry and Jessie smiled at each other at the word *lambs*.

"Nothing for us," called Henry.

"I need some brown thread, please," called Violet.

"A dog," called Benny.

Mama smiled her big smile. Papa waved.

"Take care of one another," called Mama. "You know how to do that."

And they were off.

Waves of summer heat rose off the land. Henry and Jessie watched them over the big meadow.

"No. Not fall yet," Jessie said.

Henry and Jessie took cool water to Betty and Boots.

"I could swim in a nice pond," said Henry.

"I could eat a nice sandwich," said Jessie.

When they went inside, Violet was feeding Benny.

"Mama made fresh bread. Three loaves," said Violet.

"Is there chocolate?" asked Benny.

"You wish for good things, Benny," said Jessie.

"I always wish for good things," said Benny.

"Even when they aren't there," said Violet with a smile. "Let's go write a letter to William and Meg, Benny. You can draw a picture."

"I drew a picture of Betty," said Benny. "Meg misses Betty."

Henry grinned at Jessie when they were gone.

"Have you seen his Betty picture?" he asked.

Jessie shook her head.

"It is part horse, part cow," said Henry.

"That's our Betty," said Jessie.

There was the sound of a car in the driveway.

Henry went to the window.

"Jess? It's Sheriff Bowen," Henry said slowly.

The sheriff got out of the car. Rubin got out of the driver's side.

"Something's wrong," said Henry in a low voice. "You stay with Violet and Benny."

Jessie looked out the window, too.

"No," she said. "I'll go out with you."

Henry took a deep breath.

"Okay."

They walked out of the door and across the yard.

"Hello," said Henry.

"Hello, Henry," said the sheriff. "Jessie."

His face was very still.

Henry and Jessie looked at each other.

They knew.

They knew in that moment.

It was Rubin who told them.

"There's been an accident," he said. "A bad accident."

He touched Henry's arm.

"They are gone," said Rubin, beginning to cry.

Henry didn't cry because Rubin was crying.

Jessie made a small sound that caused Henry to reach for her hand.

Sheriff Bowen cleared his throat as if it was hard to talk.

"It was a car accident," he said. "A truck went through a stop sign."

His voice trailed off.

"Someone has to take care of you," he said.

Henry looked quickly at him.

"What do you mean?"

"A relative," said Sheriff Bowen. "A family member. You must have someone."

Jessie and Henry didn't say anything.

"Otherwise . . ." Sheriff Bowen stopped for a moment. "Otherwise . . ."

"Tom!" said Rubin. "We'll solve this without that. I can stay with them."

"You're not family, Rubin," said Sheriff Bowen. "The court wants family."

"Belle and I will stay with them," said Rubin in a strong voice.

"Wait," Henry said softly.

A little wind came up. Jessie's hair blew against her cheek.

"We have a grandfather," said Henry.

Jessie looked quickly at Henry.

"I'll contact him today," said Henry.

"We can do that for you," said the sheriff. "What is his name? Where does he live?"

"No," said Henry firmly. "I want to do it. They were . . . They *are* our parents."

Sheriff Bowen sighed.

"All right, then. I'll stop by tomorrow afternoon to make sure he's coming to get you."

"We'll watch over them tonight," said Rubin.

The sheriff nodded and started to walk to

his car, then turned.

"I'm awfully sorry, Jessie, Henry. I am so, so sorry." His voice was soft.

"Thank you," said Jessie.

Henry nodded.

The sheriff reached into this pocket and walked back to them.

"I forgot. This was found in the front seat of the car."

He handed Jessie a small object.

It was a small spool of brown thread.

❧

The wind had stilled. The sun was over the far meadow. Rubin had gone home, promising to come back later with dinner. Jessie and Henry had watched him leave. He reached out over the fence to stroke Betty, then Boots. He looked back at them once. His eyes were sad and dark.

"What will we do?" whispered Jessie.

She didn't know why she whispered. Maybe it was because all that had happened was too sad to talk about out loud.

"We aren't calling Grandfather," said Henry.

"But you said—" Jessie began.

"I know. We need time. We can't rely on Grandfather taking care of us."

"Even after what Papa said? That we would see him one day?" Jessie asked.

"We don't know if he would want to take care of us now. We don't know him. Rubin can't take care of us. The law says."

Henry looked at Jessie.

"And I don't want to think about what the sheriff meant by 'otherwise,' and Rubin wouldn't let him say."

"Do you know what he meant?" asked Jessie.

Henry nodded.

"The children's home," he said. "For orphans."

Jessie stared at him.

"We have to take care of ourselves," Henry said. "We know how to do that. Remember? Mama said."

Henry's voice cracked a bit.

Jessie thought for a moment.

"We're going to leave," said Jess.

"Yes."

Slowly they walked to the house.

Suddenly Jessie stopped.

"What?" said Henry.

"We have to tell Violet and Benny," said Jessie, beginning to cry for the very first time.

Chapter 13

Secrets

"What will we do?" asked Violet.

"It's a big, big secret," said Henry. "Can you keep a secret?"

"I can," said Violet.

"We're going on a journey," said Henry. "A journey?"

"Yes, we're going to find a safe place for us away from here. A place where we can all be together."

"Do we have to leave here?" asked Violet, tears sitting in the corners of her eyes.

"Yes," said Jessie.

"Then it will be an adventure," said Violet. "Remember, Henry? You once wanted an adventure."

Henry swallowed.

"I remember."

"Travelers," Violet said quietly.

Benny was sleeping, clutching his brown stuffed bear. No one was sure if Benny really understood what had happened. But what he did understand had made him tired.

"We'll have to take special care of Benny," said Jessie. "He's so little."

"We'll have to pack some clothes for him. And food. Just a few toys," said Violet.

"I'll have to carry him sometimes," said Henry. "We'll be walking."

"Henry?" said Jessie suddenly. "What about Betty and Boots?"

Henry looked out the window.

"I'll go see Rubin right now. We have to trust him."

"Want me to come?" asked Jessie.

Henry shook his head.

"Benny will need you when he wakes up."

And Benny did.

After Henry left, Benny came out of the bedroom, carrying Bear. He climbed up on Jessie's lap—so silent, no words. Just laying his head on Jessie's shoulder.

Jessie didn't say anything, either. She just held him, the afternoon light coming through the open door, the house as still as night.

❧

"Rubin?"

In the field, Rubin turned and walked over.

"Henry."

Rubin put his arms around Henry and they stood quietly in the grasses.

"Want to come in and see Belle?"

Henry shook his head.

"Not now," he said.

Rubin nodded.

"What about your grandfather?"

Henry sighed.

"I don't want to lie to you, Rubin."

Rubin smiled a small smile.

"Then I won't ask," he said.

"I came to ask you to please take Betty and Boots," said Henry, "if you can."

"I can do that. I owe your Papa for hay, too," he said.

"The money isn't as important as the cows," said Henry.

Rubin nodded.

"I'll take care of them."

"Until we get back," said Henry.

"Get back," said Rubin.

It wasn't a question.

"Thank you," said Henry.

Henry turned to leave, then stopped. He just looked at Rubin for a moment, as if trying to remember how he looked.

"You'll miss their funeral," said Rubin.

Henry nodded.

"I know that you will say good things about them," Henry said. "You loved them."

"I did," said Rubin.

"We loved them, too," said Henry. "They

knew that."

Henry looked at his feet in the meadow grasses for a moment. Then he looked at Rubin.

"Good-bye, Rubin," he said.

Rubin watched Henry walk away.

"Good-bye," whispered Rubin.

Chapter 14

Lambs

Henry and Jessie hadn't thought about dinner. But Belle had. She brought a stew and put it on the stove and heated it for them. She set the table without saying anything. Belle didn't talk very much.

"Thank you, Belle," said Henry.

She looked at him. She took some money from her pocket and handed it to him.

"From Rubin. He owed your father," she said.

"Thank you," said Henry.

"You'll be fine," she said.

"Yes," said Henry. "We will."

Belle started to cry then.

Benny put his arms around Belle's waist.

"Don't cry, Belle," he said, which made her cry more. "I'll draw you a picture. And we'll come back."

Belle wiped her eyes.

"I will wait for that," she said.

She looked at all of them and went to the door.

"I'll come clean up tomorrow and pick up my stew pot," she said. She opened the door and looked back at them once.

"You'll be fine," she repeated.

They ate silently, early, while there were still hours of light yet.

It was after dinner that Benny disappeared.

❧

"Benny! Henry, is Benny with you?" called Jessie.

Henry ran inside the house.

"No. Where's Violet?"

"I'll check all the bedrooms," said Jessie.

"I'll look for Violet," said Henry.

"Violet! Violet!"

Violet came around the house.

"I'm here."

"Where's Benny? Have you seen him?"

Henry's voice didn't sound like his voice. He couldn't remember ever being so frightened.

Violet shook her head.

"Where should I look?" she said.

"Go through the barn, then out in the field. Maybe he went to Rubin's."

Jessie came out of the house. She shook her head.

"Not inside," she said.

Her eyes were big.

"It's going to get dark in another hour," she said. "We have to find him."

Together they searched their meadow and down by the stream that trickled there. They called his name over and over.

"Benny! Benny!"

"He couldn't go much farther than this,"

said Jessie.

They turned back. It had been an hour. Benny had never been gone for an hour. Benny had never been gone at all.

And then they saw Violet waving to them at the edge of the meadow. Beside her was a small figure. *Benny!*

Henry grabbed Jessie's hand, and they ran. Benny looked tired.

"I found him in the barn hideaway. Sleeping. He never heard us calling," said Violet.

Henry took Benny in his arms and they walked back to the house.

No one spoke.

There were no words.

❧

Jessie slept with Benny and Benny's bear.

"I should help you with the packing," Jessie said in a low voice.

"Benny needs you," Henry whispered to her in the darkness. "Having you near will make it easier for him."

"Having us *all* together will make it easier for him," said Jessie. "For all of us," she added. "We can't lose Benny again."

"Remember? Mama called us lambs before she left?" said Violet from the other bed. "She said to take care of one another."

"Violet, you'd better go to sleep," said Jessie. "Tomorrow's a long day."

Henry sat on Violet's bed.

He held her hand.

"You're right, Violet. We do know how to do this. We will be a little herd of lambs."

"And I will be the fixer lamb," said Violet, yawning.

"You will," said Henry.

Benny turned over in bed.

"Jessie?" he cried out.

"I'm here, Benny. Go to sleep now."

"I will," said Benny, already partway back to sleep.

"Good night, Jess," said Henry, touching Jessie's hair. "I'll be through with the packing soon."

"Good night, Henry."

At the doorway to the bedroom, Henry turned.

"We'll be all right, Jess."

"Yes," whispered Jessie. "Remember, Mama once told us we were the best family of all."

∾⌇∾

They all ate breakfast in sunlight.

"It's almost too bright," Jessie whispered to Henry. "Too cheerful."

"It's better for Violet and Benny," said Henry.

The food was packed. The clothes were packed.

"We can pack one very small bag of things you want to take," said Jessie to Violet and Benny. "Only one bag. And we'll have to carry it."

"Remember William and Meg," said Henry.

"I'll take my sewing bag—the little screwdriver Jake gave me," said Violet. "And the spool of brown thread," she added in a soft voice. She looked at her Mama's chipped cup on the windowsill.

"I can't take that," she whispered.

"You can if you can carry it," said Henry. He smoothed her hair.

He watched Violet wrap the mended cup in a shirt and put it in her bag.

"I'll carry the bag of clothes and food," he said.

"We have the bread, some cheese, and fruit," said Jessie. "Belle left biscuits and cookies."

"May I take Bear?" asked Benny.

"Yes," said Jessie.

Benny smiled and Jessie smiled, too.

"Bear will like the venture," said Benny.

"Adventure," corrected Violet.

"Then let's clean up and go," said Henry.

Benny ran into the bedroom and came back with a paper. It was a drawing of four children, from tall to little.

"I promised Belle," he said, putting it on the table.

"That is us," Benny added with a smile.

Jessie put her arm around Benny.

"It is us," she said, her voice soft.

Henry looked at the turn-around globe sitting in the middle of the kitchen table.

"Do you know which way we're going?" asked Jessie.

Henry nodded.

"We'll go back roads away from town so nobody we know sees us."

Violet pointed at a spot on the globe.

"That's where Sarah and Jake live," she said.

"And William and Meg. And Joe," said Benny. "Could we go there?"

"Maybe. It's a longer journey than it looks, Benny," said Henry. "But we will be together, the four of us, no matter what. We'll take care of each other. And maybe one day we'll visit them."

"Get the money in the cookie jar," said Jessie, "and Jake and Sarah's address, so we have it," she whispered.

"Now." Henry looked around the room. "Pick up what you're taking. And we will begin our . . ."

"Adventure!" said Benny.

They went out the door and up through the yard.

"Good-bye, Betty! Good-bye, Boots!" said Benny.

Boots didn't look up, but Betty watched them as they walked across the yard and up to the road in sunlight.

They walked past the sign that said Fair Meadow Farm and down the road, Henry and Jessie in front, Violet and Benny behind them. Four lambs.

They walked quietly until soon the Alden farm was out of sight. After a while they passed houses and meadows and streams they had never seen before.

When Jessie looked back she saw that Violet and Benny were holding hands.

Jessie looked sideways at Henry. Then she reached out and took Henry's hand to let him know, in her own quiet way, that it was all right that tears came down his face.

Henry squeezed her hand.
The four lambs were on their way.

AFTERWORD

Setting the Scene

It was a pleasure to write what I call the "beginning before the beginning" of the Boxcar Children stories by Gertrude Chandler Warner.

I love these children—Henry, Jessie, Violet, and Benny Alden. To be able to comfort one another and share the adventure of making a home in a boxcar has long been exciting for many child readers.

They are independent, intelligent, inventive, kind, and caring toward each other—the true qualities that make their little family work. I admire the strengths and bravery that they developed from being all on their own.

I tried to show these qualities in the Aldens as they lived their peaceful, full life in the months before they set off on their journey.

Before I began writing the book, I visited Gertrude Chandler Warner's hometown of Putnam, Connecticut, where she lived her whole life. The Boxcar Children Museum is there, too, alongside the train tracks, inside a real boxcar! I learned much about how a boxcar feels and looks and what it would have been like for the children to live there. I hope all readers visit the museum, either online or in person.

Ms. Warner was an elementary school teacher in Putnam for many years, and she often shared her stories with her students including her stories about the Aldens. I had the chance to meet with some of her former students during my visit to Connecticut, and they spoke glowingly about her kindness to them during their early school years.

I hope that this story of the Aldens of Fair Meadow Farm sets the scene for all the stories that follow.

—Patricia MacLachlan

Acknowledgements

I'd like to thank Fred Hedenberg and Barbara Scalise for their wealth of information about the Gertrude Chandler Warner Boxcar Children Museum in Putnam, Connecticut. Thanks also to Bob Viens, who lives in Ms. Warner's grandfather's house in Putnam.

I appreciate the enthusiasm of Ms. Warner's students from 1942 and their warm memories about her. They are John Champeau, Roger Franklin, Edeo Clark, Julia Duquette, Dorothy Defillipo, and Sandra Ames. Also, Geraldine Tetreault, Eileen Bourque, and John Millard Alvord.

An excerpt from
THE BOXCAR CHILDREN
by Gertrude Chandler Warner
Available at book stores everywhere

The story of the Alden children continues in *The Boxcar Children*. After the book was published in 1942, readers asked for more stories, and Warner wrote eighteen more books about the Aldens' adventures.

I—The Four Hungry Children

ONE WARM NIGHT four children stood in front of a bakery. No one knew them. No one knew where they had come from.

The baker's wife saw them first, as they stood looking in at the window of her store. The little boy was looking at the cakes, the big boy was looking at the loaves of bread, and the two girls were looking at the cookies.

Now the baker's wife did not like children. She did not like boys at all. So she came to the front of the bakery and listened, looking very cross.

"The cake is good, Jessie," the little boy said. He was about five years old.

"Yes, Benny," said the big girl. "But bread is better for you. Isn't it, Henry?"

"Oh, yes," said Henry. "We must have some bread, and cake is not good for Benny and Violet."

"I like bread best, anyway," said Violet. She was about ten years old, and she had pretty brown hair and brown eyes.

"That is just like you, Violet," said Henry, smiling at her. "Let's go into the bakery.

Maybe they will let us stay here for the night."

The baker's wife looked at them as they came in.

"I want three loaves of bread, please," said Jessie.

She smiled politely at the woman, but the woman did not smile. She looked at Henry as he put his hand in his pocket for the money. She looked cross, but she sold him the bread.

Jessie was looking around, too, and she saw a long red bench under each window of the bakery. The benches had flat red pillows on them.

"Will you let us stay here for the night?" Jessie asked. "We could sleep on those benches, and tomorrow we would help you wash the dishes and do things for you."

Now the woman liked this. She did not like to wash dishes very well. She would like to have a big boy to help her with her work.

"Where are your father and mother?" she asked.

"They are dead," said Henry.

"We have a grandfather in Greenfield, but we don't like him," said Benny.

Jessie put her hand over the little boy's mouth before he could say more.

"Oh, Benny, keep still!" she said.

"Why don't you like your grandfather?" asked the woman.

"He is our father's father, and he didn't like our mother," said Henry. "So we don't think he would like us. We are afraid he would be mean to us."

"Did you ever see him?" asked the woman.

"No," answered Henry.

"Then why do you think he would be mean to you?" asked the woman.

"Well, he never came to see us," said Henry. "He doesn't like us at all."

"Where did you live before you came here?" asked the woman.

But not one of the four children would tell her.

"We'll get along all right," said Jessie. "We want to stay here for only one night."

"You may stay here tonight," said the woman at last. "And tomorrow we'll see what we can do."

Henry thanked her politely.

"We are all pretty tired and hungry," he said.

The children sat down on the floor. Henry cut one of the loaves of bread into four pieces with his knife, and the children began to eat.

"Delicious!" said Henry.

"Well, I never!" said the woman.

She went into the next room and shut the door.

"I'm glad she is gone," remarked Benny, eating. "She doesn't like us."

"Sh, Benny!" said Jessie. "She is good to let us sleep here."

After supper the children lay down on their red benches, and Violet and Benny soon went to sleep.

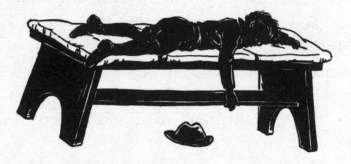

But Jessie and Henry could hear the woman talking to the baker.

She said, "I'll keep the three older children. They can help me. But the little boy must go to the Children's Home. He is too little. I cannot take care of him."

The baker answered, "Very well. Tomorrow I'll take the little boy to the Children's

Home. We'll keep the others for awhile, but we must make them tell us who their grandfather is."

Jessie and Henry waited until the baker and his wife had gone to bed. Then they sat up in the dark.

"Oh, Henry!" whispered Jessie. "Let's run away from here!"

"Yes, indeed," said Henry. "We'll never let Benny go to a Children's Home. Never, never! We must be far away by morning, or they will find us. But we must not leave any of our things here."

Jessie sat still, thinking.

"Our clothes and a cake of soap and towels are in the big laundry bag," she said. "Violet has her little workbag. And we have two loaves of bread left. Have you your knife and the money?"

"Yes," said Henry. "I have almost four dollars."

"You must carry Benny," said Jessie. "He will cry if we wake him up. But I'll wake Violet.

"Sh, Violet! Come! We are going to run away again. If we don't run away, the baker will take Benny to a Children's Home in the morning."

The little girl woke up at once. She sat up and rolled off the bench. She did not make any noise.

"What shall I do?" she whispered softly.

"Carry this," said Jessie. She gave her the workbag.

Jessie put the two loaves of bread into the laundry bag, and then she looked around the room.

"All right," she said to Henry. "Take Benny now."

Henry took Benny in his arms and carried him to the door of the bakery. Jessie took the laundry bag and opened the door very softly. All the children went out quietly. They did not say a word. Jessie shut the door, and then they all listened. Everything was very quiet. So the four children went down the street.

Resources

The Classic First Book
The Boxcar Children: Special Edition
By Gertrude Chandler Warner.
The classic story with original 1942
illustrations by L. Kate Deal.
Includes a preface by Barbara Elleman, biographical
information about Warner, and photos.
Albert Whitman & Company, 2009.

Gertrude Chandler Warner's Biography
Gertrude Chandler Warner and the Boxcar Children
by Mary Ellen Ellsworth.
Albert Whitman & Company, 1997.

The Gertrude Chandler Warner
Boxcar Children Museum
Located in Putnam, Connecticut, on South Main
Street near Union Square. The Museum is open
on weekends from May through October and
is housed in an authentic 1920s railroad boxcar.
boxcarchildrenmuseum.com

Theatrical Adaptation
The Boxcar Children, adapted by Barbara Field.
Originally produced by Seattle Children's Theatre;
scripts available through Plays for Young Audiences.
playsforyoungaudiences.org

Official Web Site
Includes a complete catalog of the books
as well as teacher guides and activities.
boxcarchildren.com

Facebook
Facebook.com/boxcarchildren

Twitter
@boxcarchildren

THE BOXCAR CHILDREN

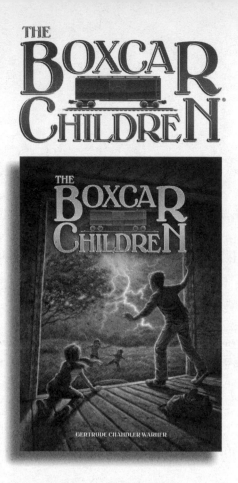

#1 THE BOXCAR CHILDREN
THE BOXCAR CHILDREN® MYSTERIES

HC 978-0-8075-0851-0
$15.99/$17.99 Canada
PB 978-0-8075-0852-7
$5.99/$6.99 Canada

*"One warm night four children stood in front
of a bakery. No one knew them. No one knew
where they had come from."* So begins Gertrude
Chandler Warner's beloved story about four
orphans who run away and find shelter in an
abandoned boxcar. There they manage to live all
on their own, and at last, find love and security
from an unexpected source.

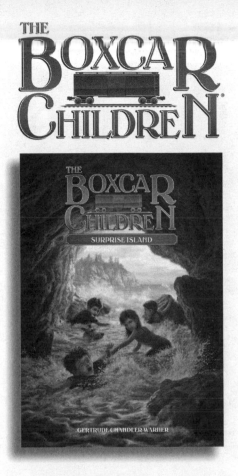

#2 SURPRISE ISLAND
THE BOXCAR CHILDREN® MYSTERIES
HC 978-0-8075-7673-1
$15.99/$17.99 Canada
PB 978-0-8075-7674-8
$5.99/$6.99 Canada
The Boxcar Children have a home with their
grandfather now—but their adventures are just
beginning! Their first adventure is to spend the
summer camping on their own private island.
The island is full of surprises, including a kind
stranger with a secret.

#3 THE YELLOW HOUSE MYSTERY
THE BOXCAR CHILDREN® MYSTERIES
HC 978-0-8075-9365-3
$15.99/$17.99 Canada
PB 978-0-8075-9366-0
$5.99/$6.99 Canada
Henry, Jessie, Violet, and Benny Alden discover
that a mystery surrounds the rundown yellow
house on Surprise Island. The children find a
letter and other clues that lead them to the trail
of a man who vanished from the house.

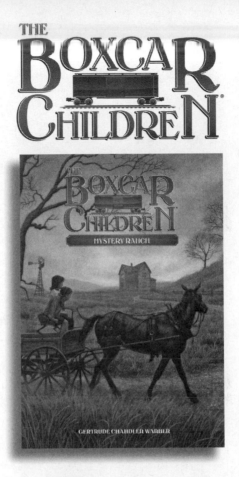